www.LittleBarnPress.com

Dedicated to all my
four-legged family members,
past and present.

Thanks for the privilege of
loving you....
Nestle, Hunter, Yogi, Petey,
Oreo, Buddy, Miley, Gucci,
Wrigley, Shelby, Tootsie Roll,
Trixi, Bailey, Peanut, Flex,
Daisy, Lexi, Whinney and
my little Noodles.

Please remember to always
rescue, and help save a life.

Sherri

Publishing this book has been my lifelong dream. Special thanks to my parents who have always taught me to reach for the stars.
Also, my dear friend Karen Perna. Thank you for designing my book, including kooky countless hours of edits on FaceTime!

Oodles About Noodles

Sherri Levy Wolff

Hey guys...
Gather round.
My name is Noodles,
and I was just found.

I was scared and alone,
  living on the streets.
It was summer
  in Florida,
and that's some
  serious heat.

I'm a tiny Chihuahua.
I weigh just 5 pounds.

A nice lady found me,
and now
I'm loved mounds.

She ran a small rescue,
    with dogs, cats and fish.
She posted my picture.
    I waited... I wished.

Many weeks later,
I don t remember the day.
I can picture her face though,
and what she did say.

She pointed.
She smiled.
And I knew it was true.
My mom had just
found me.
I would
no longer
be blue!

Mom brought me home and what did I see?
I had a new brother as sweet as can be.
And his name is Wrigley.

We like to stare at each other.
It's a game that we play.
Who ever blinks first,
is the loser that day.

I love to go for walks.
   It's my favorite thing to do.
I can walk for miles and miles.
      Wrigley always comes too!

This is my new bag.
Mom found it for me.

We go on adventures.
Far as my eyes can see.

My favorite place to go,
     is hands down
              T.J. Mutts.

They sell
     dog toys
and cookies.

I get so crazy,
     I drive
          Mom nuts!

T·J·MUTTS

I found my cute
    elephant there.
    I named her Maggie May.
        She's pink, soft and fluffy.
            Hip hip hooray!!!

I have lots of friends,
two-legged and four.
My best friend is Gypsy.
There are none I love more.

You should see all my clothes:
blue, green, brown and red.
My soft yellow pajamas,
are my favorites for bed.

So there you have it.
My poem is all done.
If you see a pup out there,
remember don't run.
He or she may be scared, lonely or alone.
Ask someone to help you.
Someone big and all grown.

The End

♥ Noodles

CPSIA information can be obtained
at www.ICGtesting.com
Printed in the USA
BVHW022352160920
588954BV00023BA/438

9 781087 860497